About the Author

Andrew Daniels is a native of Washington, also known as "The Evergreen State" for its lush evergreen forests. He was born in 1992 of Irish-Cherokee-German descent. At age nine, Andrew won the 53rd Annual Kids Fishing Derby hosted by the Tacoma Sportsmen's Club in 2002.

He attended Lincoln High School as a teenager where he excelled in literature, as well as making people laugh. While a student there, he earned two varsity letters after joining the school golf team. Andrew graduated from Lincoln High School in June of 2011 after being recognized as a scholar athlete that season.

Sticks and Stones Falling from the Sky

Andrew Daniels

Sticks and Stones Falling from the Sky

Olympia Publishers

London

www.olympiapublishers.com
OLYMPIA PAPERBACK EDITION

Copyright © Andrew Daniels 2017

The right of Andrew Daniels to be identified as author of this work has been asserted in accordance with sections 77 and 78 of the Copyright, Designs and Patents Act 1988.

All Rights Reserved

No reproduction, copy or transmission of this publication may be made without written permission.
No paragraph of this publication may be reproduced, copied or transmitted save with the written permission of the publisher, or in accordance with the provisions of the Copyright Act 1956 (as amended).

Any person who commits any unauthorised act in relation to this publication may be liable to criminal prosecution and civil claims for damage.
A CIP catalogue record for this title is available from the British Library.
ISBN: 978-1-84897-899-7
This is a work of fiction.
Names, characters, places and incidents originate from the writer's imagination. Any resemblance to actual persons, living or dead, is purely coincidental.
First Published in 2017
Olympia Publishers
60 Cannon Street
London
EC4N 6NP
Printed in Great Britain

Dedication

This is for God and everybody named Andrew.

One more thing, why did the police chase the clown?

He decided to run for president.

Acknowledgments

I would like to thank my associates from Olympia Publishers residing in Great Britain for their kindness and careful consideration of my poetry. Thanks to their wonderful work, the world has the opportunity to read my inspiration.

I thank my executive editor James Houghton for his support and constructive advice.

I thank Chantelle Wadsworth for providing her marketing and promotional skills.

I thank Mia Turner for producing the brilliant cover of my work.

I thank Gwyneth Allen for assisting me with royalty information and accounts.

I thank Mark Marlowe for giving my poetry the opportunity to be published.

I would also like to thank Claremont Graduate University for providing the prestigious Kingsley and Kate Tufts Poetry Awards to devout poets like myself.

I strongly thank my mother and father for teaching me to be a light in this world and lead the way.

Let's Burn Rubber Baby!

When I think of a woman, I think of you.
When you think of a man, do you think of me too?

If you were my woman, I would be your car.
Your love drives me crazier than a hotrod and faster than a shooting star.

The gears in my heart shift when you step on my brake.
The wheels of my heart spin when you start my engine.

You fill my flat tires with love.
My heart runs on your kindness.

When I break down, your love and kindness build me back up.
Your love is the key to the engine of my heart throbbing with secrets no other key could unlock and a motor no other love could start.

My heart races as your love accelerates to me so sweet from the sour start.
My heart cheers as your love speeds through the finish line of my throbbing heart.

When someone else finished the race to your heart, lemons rained from the sky.

Lemons fell as I dreamt about you day and night.

Red lights and stop signs could not stop my love from reaching you.
Speed limits and speed bumps could not slow my love speeding to you.

I print the letters of my license plates with the name of love.
Step behind the wheel of my heavy-duty heart and get ready for the ride of your life.

As you light my engine on fire and shift my gear into groovy, let's make that fire spin, let's burn rubber baby!

Autumn

Leaves are changing.
Leaves are falling.
Leaves are abandoning the awakening autumn tree.

Leaves are partly green as red and yellow are slowly seen.
Leaves are falling to the calling of a blossoming deity whose name is Autumn.

Her elegant silk dress elegantly flows the color of faded limes, flowing the aroma of rose petals and rose vines.

Her hair, long as time and black as night.
Falling autumn leaves color her crown with morning sunshine.

Autumn's leaves. Autumn's trees. Autumn's breeze.
These are her followers and protectors, her loyal servants and loving children.

I see reflections of autumn in her eyes.
I feel alive through her seasonal touch.
I hear her mellow voice sway through autumn branches in an autumn breeze.

Her eyes green as grass, two emeralds sparkling the beauty of a blossoming goddess.

Her laughter is music causing autumn to dance and sing.

Her crown of golden light sparkles a rainbow of diamonds.

The autumn tree is her throne sitting between summer and winter.
She blows her love west to melt winter frost off autumn leaves.
She blossoms her beauty south to seduce summer with autumn trees.

Autumn raises the sun at dawn and raises the moon at dusk.
Autumn harvests peaches and pears at dawn, harvesting golden wheat at dusk.

The sun and moon bow before Autumn, kissing her hand.
Autumn is here as autumn trees appear.
She is the season of shedding the life we once grew and beginning anew.

The Knight

A knight grips his onyx sword, unsheathing his courage to defend his code.
The knight is sworn to honor and sworn to valor.

He is a leader of protectors and a leader of defenders.
The Knight's Code of Chivalry is written onto his shield and forged into his honor.

Adorned with red lions of bravery and blue horses of loyalty, the knight unsheathes his blade of courage and leads his clad in courage cavalry.

The knight, clad in the armor of royalty and the armor of loyalty leads his cavalry clad in honor and fearless might.

Horses thunder across the field into battle.
The knight rides with honor in silence, fearlessly charging into a storm of steel as the war trumpets sound.
Fearless and valiant the knight's cavalry gallop the ground.

Barbarian warriors clash with the iron horsemen.
The knight wields an iron will no barbarian can bend and a code no barbarian can break.

The knight and his cavalry of lions stain the battlefield red.

The knight and his cavalry quickly bring the barbarian clan to a barbaric end.

The knight's courage was not shed in vain.
Barbarian warriors lay silent, lay slain.

The barbarians meet a brutal end.
The knight's blade brutally stained.
His code triumphantly sounds across the battlefield.

Horses mounted, the fights slain are counted.
The knight and his cavalry, crowned with a victory they will wear forever.

The Stairway to Heaven

The end of the road is an empty pocket of time paved with
the finger of the past that wrote history itself.

We walk down the road called life, learning a thing or two
about the beginning and the end.

We learn the dark truth we have known since the beginning.
The beginning is a thief who will steal the time we save in
our pocket.

The end is a lie, wrapping its words around the truth and
tearing it apart.

Our tears are a sea of sorrow.
We swim in despair.

We silently scream.
We pray day and night.

The beginning points and laughs at our pain.
The end points and laughs at our tears.

Love hears our screams.
Love hears our prayers.

Love sees our tears and records each one in its book.
Love gives us something the end of the road never will, hope.

Do not let go.
Do not give up.
Do not give in.

When the end of the road coughs up the lie that no one loves you do not let this roadblock stop you from following your dream.

The end of the road is trouble in paradise.
Love is lighter than a feather and heavier than gold.
The most powerful words in the universe start with love and end with love.

Follow your dreams and one day you will reach the end of the rainbow.
Time is running out.

When we finally learn to love, that will be the beginning of the end when love is the stairway to Heaven.

The Dirty Thirties

When nickels and dimes met gloves and greed in a boxing ring, a brawl between freedom and poverty took place during a time known as the Dirty Thirties.

Wall Street crashed stocks and bonds as the wealthy met poverty.
Wall Street crashed stocks and bonds as greed drove the Dirty Thirties into a dust bowl.

A Great Depression of hope and tears arose.
A Great Depression arose in a boxing ring with a broken heart and a broken nose.

In Hoover Ville, a fire burning in the heart of a boxer named Dirty Harry fights anyone who tries to put it out, a fire hungry for the things money can't buy.

On Wall Street a boxer named Money Max carries a heart heavy with greed and a heart heavy with pride, the two boxing gloves his heart wears.

As Hoover Ville meets Wall Street in a boxing ring, freedom and poverty will throw gloves left and right as two boxers bounce the Dirty Thirties into the limelight.

Dirty Harry is a cloud throwing thunder as Money Max hides his face behind his pride and his greed.

Money Max fights dirty, bribing the referee, cheating his way to victory as round one begins.

He breaks every rule in the book, throwing dirty words with his dirty mouth until Wall Street defeats Hoover Ville.

The crowd cheers.
The crowd boos.

The bell rings as both men go to their corners battered and bruised.
One of these men will achieve the victory.
One of these men will admit defeat.

The Dirty Thirties are a storm of bones only money can break.
Round two begins as both men stare fiercely into each other's soul.
Round two ends as both men spin wildly out of control.

Money Max staggers blind with pain, the fire burning inside Dirty Harry throws one last strike knocking Money Max and Wall Street out for the count.

The count is over as Dirty Harry is declared the new champion.

Cameras flash.
History is born.
Dirty Harry shares his victory with Hoover Ville.

The match may be over, but the flame burning inside Dirty Harry will never fade.

Wall Street will always say it doesn't matter whether we are rich or poor the only color that matters is green.

The Dirty Thirties taught us it doesn't matter whether we are rich or poor it is making sure the fire burning inside us never stops burning.

Multiple Choice Test

The clock has broken its promise.
There is no sand left in the hourglass.

My cup is empty of hope.
It all spilled on the ground as I tripped the finish line.

My compass is just as confused as I am.
I roll the dice in this guessing game of survival.

The pen I found many years ago has run out of ink.
It seems I have run out of luck since this multiple choice test stares blankly at me.

When I thought I could cheat fate, it sounded like the perfect escape.
I forget one rule, I can't escape responsibility.

When I struck oil with my pen, I thought I was filthy rich.
It turns out I was just filthy.

I failed the test, but I failed myself first.

What am I?

Beauty and intelligence.
Strength and laughter.

These are stairways to success.
These are stairways to nowhere.
These four bolts of steel lightning cut through the night,
striking the world.

We can't live without them.
They can't live without us.

There comes a time when the stars and everyone beneath
them must ask the question they've already asked themselves
countless times, what am I?

Am I the solution or the problem?
Am I the question or the answer?

Am I the sun or the moon in this world?
Do I have a name or am I just another number?

Am I sorrow or joy?
Am I just a grain of sand, a blade of grass, a drop of rain?

What am I?

Grass

The green fields wave back and forth in the wind.
The fresh scent of green grass takes me back to the summer of 1986.

The dry desert became green grass when the sky sent rain, whisking us back to our childhood where we spent the summer laughing in the fields.

These fields of green blades cut through the summer breeze, riding the wind to the present.
Sprouting in lands far and wide the green grass becomes tall trees.
These giants breathe fresh air into the world, standing their ground during the storm.

These giants reach for the stars day and night.
A blade of grass becomes a forest of fresh air, a sanctuary for hopelessness.

That is what we are, and that is what we must become.

My Heart Is My Guitar

My heart is my guitar.
I play it when I am sad.

I play it when I am happy.
My sorrow and joy turn into music only hearts can hear.

My heart is my quill.
I dip this phoenix feather in black fire.
I scribble my tears and laughter onto a scroll dipped in love.

My heart is my double-edged sword forged from an iron will and a fiery love, pumping with steel courage and steel honor into a bolt of lightning only my soul can wield.

My heart is a mystery.
Each day I get one step closer and one step farther from solving its riddle.

I walk through this maze, stumbling over clues to its hidden secrets and secrets to its hidden clues.

My heart is my friend.
When I laugh and cry, my heart laughs and cries with me.
When my heart laughs and cries, I laugh and cry with it.

My heart is my guitar, my quill, my sword, my mystery and my friend.

Together we are a family beating as one.

My heart sings an endless song echoing through the past, present and future.

My soul chases the shadows away in a dark world.

Waves from a Mermaid Violin

Ocean waves are thrashing and crashing.
Ocean waves are flowing and lashing.

This ocean is a paradise where I will not dwell until a
mermaid sings to me from her mermaid gills.

I stand on the reef rocks gently playing a mermaid hymn with
my violin.
I suddenly see a beautiful blue tail swim near me.

She swims up to me, smiling as I play.
I continue to make music as I smile back.
The mermaid silently smiles and watches in the ocean waves.

Closing my eyes, I carefully press my strings.
I open my eyes as the mermaid raises her bow to her violin.

In perfect harmony and perfect timing, our notes flow
together as our violins sing.

Her eyes, blue as sapphires are an ocean of love and an ocean
of beauty, two oceans splashing in the heart of a mermaid.

We play and play, day by day.
The waves move back and forth wave after wave.

Her heart sings with laughter as her eyes glisten with pearly
light.

Her black hair flows in the wind and ocean waves.
Her song of love and beauty echoes into the nearby beach shore caves.

I play faster and faster, my notes shrilling higher and higher.
The calming waves become lashing waves.
The thrashing waves become crashing waves.

My bow speeds up, the wind begins hissing and whistling.
My bow becomes a furious blur of screeching notes, a screeching blur of furious notes.

The setting horizon turns into darkness created by my stormy music.

She is no longer playing, no longer singing, no longer smiling.
Fear falls from her eyes once glistening the love in her heart when the sun was shining.

My violin stops as she sadly looks at me one last time before disappearing into the ocean.
The dark clouds hide as the sun rises over the ocean.
The storm clears as the gentle melody of sunshine calms the waves.

I return and play day after day, but she never came.
I was never the same since the first time I saw her.

Waves of loneliness, waves of sorrow and waves of love thrash in my heart forever and ever until she returns to sing on the shores of my heart.

Franken Claus

On a spooky Christmas Eve, Halloween fear meets holiday cheer.

A nightmare wrapped with a ribbon waits in Santa's toy sack, waiting to unwrap the holiday terror within.

Candy canes and jack o' lanterns will weep when Halloween marries Christmas.

Guitars and jingle bells will scream when Christmas marries Halloween.

A black and white nightmare unwraps as Santa's workshop meets Frankenstein's laboratory, a nightmare named Franken Claus.

Halloween plays spooky tunes with his guitar of bones.
Santa plays jolly jingles with his guitar of Christmas.

Pumpkin heads smash to their spooky jingles.
Black and white collides with rock and roll, smashing into a Christmas nightmare come true.

The world watches from their front row seats as Halloween unwraps this nightmare.

Christmas becomes a party about to get jolly, about to get

scary.
Franken Claus is a fairy tale and a nightmare.
He has presents for everyone in his Halloween sack that will scare everyone with holiday joy.

He will crawl down your chimney and into your dreams leaving you nightmares wrapped in Christmas cheer.

He will give your shivering soul a cloak of fire to wear for the blizzards of snow he is sending your way.

Franken Claus leaves nightmares under everyone's Christmas tree.
Whether you are naughty or nice, you're going to be scared.

At the stroke of midnight, Christmas bids Halloween goodbye.

Their black and white rock and roll ends but will snow from the sky again at the next Franken Claus.

The holidays are fun but not for everyone.
The party is over, but the nightmare has just begun.

Steel Love and Steel Faith

Steel love can lift the world with one hand and crush fear
with the other.
This iron hammer, a mallet forged from the flames of beauty
and the light of conviviality.

Faith can walk on water.
Faith can walk through solid steel.

With steel faith one can calm a storm, one can move
mountains and bend sunlight with their bare hands.

Together they are stronger than steel.
Unbendable.
Unbreakable.

These two are now one.
Together anything is possible.
Together these two become solid steel.

Together they are a brass pocket watch ticking time.
Together they share a rusty history of golden memories.

The past, present, and future.
These three hands spin around the glass face of time,
spinning a web of seconds, minutes and hours.

The past dangles back and forth, a brass chain clicking to the sound of a forgotten memory.

The watch runs out of time.
A waterfall of time pours out of a broken hourglass.
A shattered memory is all that remains.

Our rusty history is now in pieces.
Our golden memories are now forgotten.
Time keeps ticking as we run from our past and future.

Our names are written in history by the right hand of love and the left hand of faith as time gets rusty.

How to Write Poetry

The mind of a poet can weave anything into inspiration.
There are no limits.
There are no rules.

A true poet writes with their heart, mind, and soul.
These three pianos play in the head of a poet as they turn music into poetry.

We make paintings silently dance.
We make poems silently sing.

Imagination is our pencil.
Imagination is our paint brush.

Our poetry is where accidents meet coincidences.
We will tell you how we write poetry.

We throw our fishing pole into the sea of our mind.
A poem swims toward us.

We rush to our pole as a poem bites its hook.
We reel and reel until we catch it.

We don't watch our pole move around and decide we will catch that poem tomorrow.

We grasp this moment firmly because we might lose that
moment forever.

We are the blacksmiths of literature.
We take our poem out of the fire as it glows red.
We hammer our words onto a blank piece of paper.

We are a bolt of lightning screaming down from the sky.
We are the recipe for courage.
We are the flames of freedom.

When a poem sings, we listen.
Poetry is a language only we understand.
We are the only ones who can mend a broken poem.

A poem doesn't have to make sense.
It doesn't have to rhyme.
All a poem has to do is sing.

Inspiration was born when we dipped our quill into magic,
and our poetry set sail for wonder.

Many people don't read poetry because they don't
understand what it is all about.

The wonders we write are the wonders you read when we
strike gold with our pencil.

Lightning strikes our poetry, shattering it to pieces.
Love strikes our poetry, welding the pieces back together.

Our poem has no beginning.
Our poem has no ending.

Our words will move mountains.
Our armies are the thunder and lightning, the wind and rain.

Poems are the diamonds sparkling in a poet's heart.
Poetry is the sound of silence, the skeleton key unlocking our hopes and dreams.

Every poet is a unique reflection of inner beauty.
Every poet paints a different picture with a bolt of lightning.

If you can turn love into inspiration, you are a poet.
When your words ring like liberty bells from the tallest tower, your dreams set sail for the future.

As you look inside your heart, what kind of poem will you paint?

Checkmate

Chess board laid.
Chess players set.

The game begins.
The price of defeat is a steep price to pay.

My pieces are white.
His pieces are black.
My pieces engage as his pieces attack.

Safe behind their infantry of pawns.
Guarded by their cavalry of knights.
Kings and queens silently watch as knights and pawns savagely fight.

I inch my pawns across a battlefield of squares, a battlefield our rivalry continually clashes on.

While keeping my thoughts to myself, I remember what my mistakes of the past have harshly taught.

White pawns engage black.
Black pawns invade white.
A fierce battle of silence.

I sit in silence, making my move only when golden
opportunities silently arrive.

Black and white pawns violently fall.
Every move I make is a mistake and a miracle.

My opponent begins losing confidence and power in the dark
empire of tyranny he built.

I courageously grasp the victory.
My army takes the battlefield.

His protection lost.
His time has run out.

His king and queen are royalty no more.
He has no royal servants left to count.

Our battle is not over yet.
My silent victory is close at the ready hand.

His king and queen are doomed.
My king and queen engage where they cowardly stand.

His king and queen fall, unable to defend their royal crowns.
I cheer a single word with a single meaning for my rival's
inevitable fate.

This single word is checkmate.

Gardens of Honor and Respect

The pasture has become empty with love, empty with life.
The land is fertile enough to sprout hundreds of seedlings with hard work on many nights.

Sorrow and joy fall on the bleak pasture below.
A gardener stands silently shocked at a waste of fine soil.

His bag, filled with seeds of love and seeds of life.
He immediately begins to spread seeds to the left and seeds to the right.

The gardener plants rows of buried life soon to grow fresh and pure, soon to taste the sweet and sour fruits of success.

The gardener gazes at his endless fields of seeds, his endless fields of life.
He softly touches the first seed with his green thumb, hundreds of fruit trees spring to life.

Green as the gardener's thumb, trees wave slowly in the wind as fruits begin to sprout.
Orange trees sprout oranges and peach trees sprout peaches.
The gardener strolls through gardens of fruit and slowly reaches.

Green and red apples.
Green and yellow limes.
The gardener gives fresh fruit to those with desperate needs.

Endless plains of honor and respect grow on trees for those who hunger for the sweet taste of life.
As seasons slowly pass, the fruit trees grow faster than the green grass grows.

These gardens remain fresh and pure while other gardens shed and shiver.

The gardener returns to grow gardens of love and gardens of life, abiding by a passed down proverb Mother Nature taught him long ago.
One must give honor and respect to receive honor and respect.

Whether life gives you seeds or pebbles, if you can make them grow, you have the green thumb of a gardener.

The Viking and the Samurai

The western world unsheathes an ulfberht.
The eastern world unsheathes a katana.
Two brave warriors unleash Ragnarok while the world watches.

The samurai is quick as the wind.
The Viking is tough as a stone.

The western world clashes with the eastern world.
Fire is born as an ulfberht and a katana clash in the heat of battle.

Japanese steel hammered into honor and respect, the samurai sharpens his katana with his iron heart.

Viking steel hammered into bravery by the bitter cold, the Viking sharpens his ulfberht with a Scandinavian blizzard.

As the world falls apart, the universe unsheathes a magic sword.

A sword forged with billions of stars.
A sword sharpened with the sun and moon.
A sword hammered by God into the ray of light that would save the world.

Ragnarok and Armageddon, two bolts of lightning
unleashing their anger, shaking Heaven and Earth.

The Viking and the samurai watch with awe, their hearts
heavy as their battle burns to ashes.

Both look at each other, sheathing their swords.
Shaking hands their hearts part ways, their burning battle
doused by peace.

Gift of the Silver Tongue

The gift of the silver tongue is the mark of a thief and a liar,
both cut from the same cloth, a filthy rag.

Lies, the stumbling stones flying from a silver tongue.
These are stones that cannot be called back.

These stones become boulders.
Big boulders.
Giant boulders.

Colossal boulders.
Titanic boulders.

Heavier than Earth.
Heavier than Heaven.

With a silver tongue, we can say anything except the truth.
With a silver tongue, we can hear everything except
ourselves.

A silver tongue, paved with miles of black and white lies.
A silver tongue tries to turn a lie into the truth and the truth
into a lie.

No one can bend the truth.
No one can break the truth.
The truth never changes.

It can't be hidden behind a lie forever.
The truth will search the past to find the future.
The future will search the past to find the truth.

The truth will break the shackles of lies binding it and bend the bars standing in the way.
The silver tongue becomes rusty as it spits lies in the face of the truth.

The gift of the silver tongue is a curse.
There is no escape from the jaws of a lie.
However, there is also no escaping the wrath of the truth.

Graffiti

I take a walk through my life.
I see graffiti here.

I see graffiti there.
I see graffiti everywhere.

My sins are spray painted all over my heart.
My mistakes are spray painted all over my past.

No matter how hard I scrub, I can't erase the past.
I can't erase my sins or my mistakes.

I will not try to hide my sins and mistakes behind graffiti.
No matter how much I spray, they will always be there.

I take a bolt of lightning and strike my mistakes into miracles.
I take another bolt of lightning and strike my sins into saints.
I take one more bolt of lightning and strike my graffiti into beauty.

Whenever I look in the mirror, I stare silently at myself.
My reflection stares back.
I stare into my face.

I stare into my eyes.
I see who I really am.

I see what no one else can, a miracle.

Spring, Summer and Winter

In the beginning, Mother Nature gave birth to three sons who would rain, shine and snow.

Mother Nature also gave birth to three daughters named April, August, and December.

One beginning.
One middle.
One ending.

Three melodies.
Drops of rain falling from the sky.
Rays of sunshine falling from the sun.
Flakes of snow falling from the clouds.

Three seasons.
Six days of rain drops.
Six days of sunshine.
Six days of snowflakes.

Three friends.
One crying.
One laughing.
One shivering.

Maple leaves grow in the spring.
Maple leaves dance in the summer.

Maple leaves fall in the winter.
Maple leaves blow in the four winds of a Canadian breeze.

When spring turns into summer and summer turns into winter, Nature turns into the season of seduction.

Raining love.
Shining love.
Snowing love.

I turn into the season that bows before her and kisses her hand, the season that loves her.

Lobotomy

My mind has become my prison, my asylum.
Hopelessness and confusion wander the halls of my mind where my dreams, my sanity, and my future wear a straitjacket.

My dreams attempt to escape from this nightmare as I gaze out a barred window in my mind.

The foggy fields and leafless trees are my only comfort.
Someday I might set foot on those fields of freedom.

The iron gates are the line where madness ends and madness begins, where freedom stops and freedom starts.

I no longer live in a dream called reality.
I live in the nightmare of a lobotomy, a nightmare stitched together by the hands of a madman.

He takes apart my dreams.
He takes apart my nightmares, turning my mind inside out as he stitches the pieces back together into a straitjacket for my mind.

When I set foot in this dark place madness met reality.
Right and wrong are the doctors running it.

I and my sanity live trapped in this nightmare.
We sit locked together in this asylum where time does not exist.

The world has stopped spinning, all of the clocks broke in this place long ago.
Time is currently on vacation.

Nothing makes any sense.
Nothing is real anymore.

The stitches holding my mind together are my broken dreams and worst nightmares.

These wounds are the stitches of a lobotomy.

Black and Blue

If an angel with black hair and blue eyes is reading this poem, this is a true story about me and you in a dream.

When life is black and white, you step into the picture with your big blue eyes, sparkling your black and blue beauty.

I sit in silence as you walk by, silently staring into my soul.
I cannot escape you.

Your eyes blaze with blue fire.
Your hair is a black storm.

You are a goddess among mortals, perfect in every way.
I would part the ocean just to see you smile.
I would give you all the treasure in my heart to make you happy.

Your name is a mystery.
Too beautiful to forget, too bright to see, an ocean of black and blue diamonds.

Your eyes are a galaxy of black and blue stars, a storm of black and blue lightning.

You are the wind in my hair, the storm in my mind, the bolt of lightning that struck my heart and shattered it forever.

I'm a fool to think you love me the way I love you.
You are a fireball burning in my memory.
You are a song I listen to every day in my mind, my soul and my heart.

I sit in stunned silence as you walk up and talk to me.
Your magical voice brings joy into my life.
I feel your hand slide through my hair as you lean down and kiss my forehead.

I faint from your power.
I wake up, and you are gone.
For the rest of my life, I wonder if you were a dream or a dream come true.

I'm a prisoner of love.
Your black and blue love kisses my forehead when I'm awake and when I'm dreaming.

Happy Birthday

Today is a special day.
Today is your day.

Today is the day your life began.
Today is your birthday.

Given the gift of life, a special gift given to all people.
Given gifts not yet opened only you can unwrap, only you have received.

We will take you to your favorite place, that special place you have always wished to go.
We will give you small balloons and big balloons from all the colors of the rainbow.

We will have a celebration chilled with red and white wine all day and all night.
We will celebrate your special day lit by California sunshine.

We will give you joy and happiness wrapped in love.
We will give you love wrapped in joy and happiness.

We will give you a birthday filled with hours of laughter and hours of fun.

We will gather around you lovingly and sing your song in the California sun.
Think of the things you want while the candles still glow brightly.
Wish for what you desire until the flames turn into California moonlight.

Today we celebrate your special day giving you many party favors along the way.
Today as we celebrate your special day we wish you a very happy birthday.

The Sunshine Here and the Sunshine There

The sun wakes up, peeking over the horizon.
Fire turns into the morning sunshine.
Dawn sings a song.

At the dawn of today, the sunshine smiles brightly.
The morning sunshine walks on the evening sunshine across the sky.

The sunshine sparkles on the water.
The sunshine mingles with the rain.
The sunshine disappears into the night.

Three beautiful events unfold in front of me.
Three beautiful memories I will never forget.

The sunshine rains from a fiery ruby burning in the clouds, never to be doused by night.
The sunshine here and the sunshine there is the sunshine in my heart.
The sunshine from a bottle is the sunshine spilling everywhere.
We should all drink a bottle of sunshine when our lives are gray.

We should all be a ray of sunshine when there is no sunshine in the world.

When Dwarfs Become Giants

Four dwarfs named Rock begin hammering a mountain into a giant.
Red fire burns at the center of the Earth.
Red fire hammered into a giant's bones.

These mountains of iron and fire carry the past, present, and future on their shoulders, lifting the world to higher horizons where fact meets truth.

Life is a giant through the eyes of a dwarf.
Life is dwarf through the eyes of a giant.
When life throws a curveball, giants hit a home run.

A dwarf who knows courage towers over the mountains standing in its way.

Towering over the Earth, these giants wield a spirit that touches the clouds and becomes the sky.

A thousand dwarfs who try to pull one of these giants down are a thousand fools.

When cowards try to make someone else feel smaller so they can make themselves feel bigger, they always fail.

A giant who stomps on our feelings has no conscience.
Their pride has not only crushed our spirit but their own as well.

A real giant doesn't have to step on other people.
A giant is kind to things smaller than itself.

A giant doesn't want to be a foe.
A giant wants to be a friend.
We are all dwarfs, and we are all giants.

Our footsteps get bigger every day.
Our hands reach higher and higher towards the unknown.
Our shadow stretches longer and longer as time marches on.

When boys become men and girls become women, they are no longer dwarfs.

They are giants.

Golden Snake Eyes

The past, present, and future sit around a Las Vegas card table.
A game of silence begins.
The prize is a key to our hopes and dreams.

We toss our golden snake eyes.
Our fate begins to sway left and sway right.
Our future is a house of cards only a heartbeat from collapsing.

Before long our chances are gone, our golden snake eyes have chosen our fate.
The golden snake eyes fall to the ground from our trembling hands.
We continue to hope for another chance.
The chance never came.

A Glass to Her Royal Majesty

Her Majesty Queen Elizabeth II is a wonderful lady.
Let's celebrate her milestones with a glass of wine.

The celebration begins.
Red carpets and purple tables.
Royal guests and royal cake.

The trumpets sound as her majesty rides a diamond horse
into the celebration of her Diamond Jubilee.

The trumpets sound as gold and silver bow to the Queen of
Sheba and the Queen of Italy.

Emeralds sing and rubies dance.
The Queen of Spain greets the Queen of France.

Buckingham Palace welcomes its royal guests into her
majesty's home.
Horse guards and foot guards protect the queen as if she was
solid gold.

Scottish guards play bagpipes while Irish guards tap dance.
British guards stand still as statues while Welsh guards
prance.

Seated around her majesty's table are four queens.
They are four gems in her majesty's crown and four friends in her majesty's heart.
A royal family wears one crown.
A royal family beats one heart.

The Commonwealth raise a glass of wine as her majesty takes her seat.

The queens raise their glasses.
Queen Elizabeth celebrates her day in the sun.

Remember her Gold and Silver Jubilee.
Remember her Diamond Jubilee.
Most of all remember her as we raise a glass to her royal majesty.

Long live Great Britain.

The Sun Dances with the Moon

In an endless black sea of space, the sun and the moon will swim together in a sparkling cosmos.

Two celestials will dance to the end of time.
Two diamonds will dance on galaxies of pearls.
Two lovers will dance to infinity and beyond.

For some people, the sun is their moon.
For others, the moon is their sun.

The pearly moonlight smiles in the black onyx night.
Two celestials hold each other's hand, holding each other's heart.
The sun and the moon dance through the sparkling cosmos and their love dances with them.

These two celestials stare into each other's eyes, staring into each other's soul.
Shooting stars circle them as their love circles the universe.

The sun and the moon are twins of light in the Milky Way Galaxy.

One lights the day.
One lights the night.

The sun goes to sleep.
The moon sings a lullaby to the earth, singing a sparkling waterfall of stars and diamonds into the hearts of people.

Forever in love.
Forever together.

Forever two celestials dancing to the end of time.
Forever two diamonds dancing on galaxies of pearls.
Forever two lovers dancing to infinity and beyond.

The Sapphire Salmon

A sapphire catches on the hook of a poor boy's heart.
A sapphire gets caught in the net of his life.
A sapphire swims in the depths of his dream.

He goes fishing.
He opens his heart and pulls out some fire.
He crafts the fire into a fishing pole that will catch a sapphire and a dream.

He casts his heart out, baiting his hook with his hopes and dreams.
Time splashes on the shore of his life while he silently watches his pole.

Hoping.
Dreaming.
Waiting.

A group fishers pass him by, pointing and laughing at his misfortune.

Their egos poisoned with pride hang with fish.
They throw hurtful words at the boy, leaving him in tears.

The moon casts its fishing pole into the lake.
The moon hears the sound of the boy's broken heart.

The moon kindly comforts the boy, giving him its fishing pole made from a shooting star.

The moon sparkles with kindness.
His hopes and dreams are quickly hooked as he casts the shooting star out.
Water splashes as a star and a sapphire pull at each other.

The shooting star gives the boy the strength of the seven seas.
He pulls in a sapphire.

For centuries fishers have searched for them and for centuries they have escaped them.

The boy smiles and releases the sapphire back into the lake.
The crowd gasps.

The moon winks at the boy as the sapphire swims away.
The boy caught his dream.
Or did his dream catch him?
Everyone asks why he let it go.

The boy takes the shooting star in one hand and his heart in the other.
He caught his dream with the moon's kindness, next time he will catch his dream with his heart.

The Scarecrow and the Snowman

Night becomes day.
Black crows circle the farm fields.
White crows circle the snow fields.

The scarecrow and the snowman stand silent.
The white shadow of morning ends their slumber.
Their body of straw and body of snow come to life.

The morning fog becomes a blanket of morning dew glistening on the grass.
The misty air is fresh with the scent of pine trees.

The scarecrow watches the crows fly east.
The snowman watches the crows fly west.

The scarecrow crosses the farm field to follow the black crows.
The snowman crosses the snowfield to follow the white crows.

The scarecrow and the snowman walk through frozen time.
The bitter cold is a warm cloak the snowman wears during the winter.

Winter is a journey through the fields of time.
The scarecrow spots the snowman.
The snowman stares at the scarecrow.
One stares at the other in a silence that could shatter glass.

The farm field greets the snow field.
Today and tomorrow shake hands as an old chapter ends and a new chapter begins.

The scarecrow and the snowman set sail on the most exciting adventure of all, friendship.

The Pink Pearl

I put a message in my glass heart.
I toss my heart into the ocean.
A ship called the Pink Pearl emerges.

This glass ship sails on a sea of clouds.
This glass ship sails on a sea of stars.

This ship sails on a sea of sapphire.
My glass heart rides the ocean with adventure in its pink sails.

The sun blows wind to the north.
The moon blows wind to the south.
The Pink Pearl sails on a song the ocean sings.

Hold onto hope with both hands and never let go.
This song is the Pink Pearl sailing the seven seas.
This song is the message in my glass heart.

No matter what happens, the mistakes from my past will not take the wind out of my sails.

Camera One, Camera Two

Fame and fortune are the mother and father of Hollywood.
They gave birth to every star on the sidewalk.

They directed every movie through the eye of a camera.
They sing every song on the radio.

Camera one watches fame.
Camera two watches fortune.

Fame wears leather and jeans.
Leather and jeans become gold and silver.
Gold and silver become stacks of success.

The diamonds in the sky snap pictures as fame and fortune step out of a limo.

The diamonds in the sky ask for autographs as leather and jeans walk down the red carpet.

The diamonds in the sky scream with applause as gold and silver smile for camera one and camera two.

Lights, cameras, and action become millions of dollars.
Leather and jeans become famous rock stars sparkling in the night sky.

Gold and silver catch celebrities on camera one and camera two.
History spills out of a roll of film as Hollywood turns the cameras off.

Stripes and Spots

A leopard can't change its spots.
A zebra can't change its stripes.
When spots become stripes, black becomes white, wrong becomes right and day becomes night.

When stripes are happy, every day is sunny.
When spots are sad, every day is rainy.

Spots hunt stripes in the heart of Africa.
Black and orange hunt black and white.

A leopard with hungry eyes prowls the African landscape, hungry for two zebras.
Those two zebras are you and me.

However we are not zebras, we are ninjas.
We take stars from the sky and throw them at our vicious hunter, striking his green glare with cosmic fire.

We are lions.
We hunt the hunter.
When we roar everything stops, everything trembles and everything listens.

We are leaders.
We are the beginning and the end.
The thunder, rain, and wind follow in our footsteps.

When we speak, the thunder is silent.
When we scream, the rain stops.
When we sing the wind sings with us, the storm has passed.

Everybody is either a leopard or a zebra.
Everybody is either a stripe or a spot.

Playing Hardball with God

The big game is about to begin.
The universe throws itself at me as the planets position
themselves on the field.

Mars takes first base.
Neptune takes second.

Uranus takes third.
Saturn takes fourth.
God is the pitcher.

I wear the moon over my head.
I take the sun and straighten it into a bat.
The universe watches with its eyes fixed on me.

I step up to the plate.
God hurls a meteor toward me.

I swing.
I miss.
Earth yells "Strike one!"

I tighten my grip.
God hurls a comet toward me.

I swing.
I miss.
Earth yells "Strike two!"

I don't blink.
I don't think.
I keep my eye on the ball.

God hurls a shooting star toward me.
I swing with all my might.

An explosion louder than the Big Bang shakes the universe as I hit a shooting star into a home run.

I run faster than the speed of light around the cosmic diamond.
The score is zero to infinity.

The universe cheers with silence as God spins the earth on His finger.

Three Guitars and a Pair of Drumsticks

Rock and roll gave birth to a legendary band called the Beatles.

Rock and roll gave birth to three guitars and a pair of drumsticks named
John, Paul, George, and Ringo.

They rocked the sixties.
They rocked the world with music that never gets old even when it turns sixty-four.

In a time where everything was black and white, the Beatles painted the sixties with a color no one had seen before, love.

They sing in our heads day and night.
They made songs out of love and light.

They help us when we are feeling down.
They make us smile when we want to frown.

Their voices are sweeter than strawberry wine.
The Beatles will always rock and roll in the hearts of their fans.

A million years from now the girls will still be screaming and fainting over them.

A million years from now the radio will still be twisting and shouting to their songs.

We will always remember the four lads from Liverpool that became four brothers of rock and roll.

Before Michael Jackson, there was the Beatles.
Before the Beatles there was Elvis.
Before Elvis, there was no one.

Their songs will always make the earth spin and make the earth sing.

John Lennon, Paul McCartney, George Harrison and Ringo Starr will always be the Beatles!
Yesterday, today and forever!

Broken Umbrella

There is a place in my heart where the sun never shines,
where the rain never stops.

It is the place where my shattered dreams weep, the place where my forgotten memories repeat and the place where my broken heart never sleeps.

My broken heart.
My broken umbrella.

The pieces never fit, there is no love holding them together, there is no fire to show them the light, and there is no flame to burn their pain.

This sad place in my heart is where love is an empty vase.
No family.
No friends.

These are the flowers that fill an empty vase with happiness and laughter.
My only friends are me, my reflection and my shadow.

I get down on my knees, surrounded by the sorrow of my heart.

There is no phone to call God.
There is no mailbox to send Him love.
No exit.
No escape.

I begin praying for someone to wake me up from this nightmare, someone to rescue me.

I hug my soul.
I try to speak, but nothing comes out except black empty silence.

In this empty place, God cannot hear me spill my heart out.
My spirit and my soul are forever alone in the shadow of despair.
My only company is the shadow of hope.

Maybe it will find me.
Maybe I will find it.
Maybe it doesn't matter.

For now, I will hide under my broken umbrella from the pain raining in my heart.

It is my only fortress of solitude.
It is just me, my broken heart and my broken umbrella.

A Recipe for Disaster

At the brink of madness seated around a table are a ray of rage, a drop of despair, a pinch of perfection, a slice of stupidity, a glass of greed and a leather purse overflowing with beauty.

At the brink of madness sits a recipe for disaster.
A recipe for reason is somewhere over the rainbow.

Liars can never find it.
Thieves can never steal it.
The shadows cannot hide it.

Mystery wrote this recipe.
Honest men and women search their whole lives for it.

A recipe for love was the best accident to come from a bottle of whiskey wine on a Friday night.

It takes only one drop to get drunk and only one drop to become addicted forever.

A drop of whiskey falls into a glass of wine, setting fire to our soul.

There is no bottom to a bottle of a whiskey wine.
The bottle is never empty.

A recipe for disaster is something only a man with an iron will and a steel spirit can swallow.

No one wrote it down.
There are millions of ingredients to it.
It is the mistake every chef makes in the kitchen called life.

Ask yourself one question.
Are you a recipe for a reason, a recipe for love or a recipe for disaster?

If you are one of the first two, share that recipe with the world.
If you are a disaster then just try to keep out of the world's way.

Try to make yourself invisible.
Common sense tells us when we are about to cross the line of common decency.
A person with no common sense is a disaster waiting to happen.

There is enough disaster in the world already.
It is a recipe that we should never learn.

When our train leaves the station, will people say goodbye or good riddance?

Push, Push, Push!

When a lawyer needs a lawyer, there is no such thing as justice.

A lawyer walks into a store and hears his clients complaining they don't have this and they don't have that.

The lawyer asks the one we call Justice "Why can't they just have it for the sake of having it so when other people want to have it they can have it when they want to have it?"

That is the million dollar question.
Here is the million dollar answer.

The hardest things to buy are the things money can't buy.
Friends, family, and love are a few of those things.

We are someone's father.
We are someone's mother.

We are someone's son.
We are someone's daughter.

We are someone's brother.
We are someone's sister.

We are someone's friend.
We are someone's family.

When life pushes us, we push harder.
As soon as we stop pushing, we lose.
Life is a long game of pushing back.

When life locks us in a nightmare, we obtain a secret password locked in a riddle.

We take the easy way out and ask life what the secret password is only to get an answer written in gibberish.

We stumble across a clue in the stainless steel door holding us prisoner with thirteen words forged into its lock.

These words are "Push, push, push. Push, push, push. Push, push, push, push, push, push, push!"

A button and a three digit combination stand between us and the other side.

We must push the button a specific number of times.
Three numbers between one and ten must be entered to unlock our freedom.

The answer is right here.

A Ladder to the Moon

I light a match and set the sun on fire.
The flames turn into the sunshine.

I have a pocket full of diamonds.
I take a handful and throw them into space as they become
the stars lighting the night sky.

My head tells me to write a song.
My heart tells me to sing a song.

My head tells me to read a poem.
My heart tells me to write a poem.

The clock starts turning backward but time keeps marching
forward.
Is the glass half full or half empty?
That is the question hiding behind an answer.

A billion dollars stacked on top of each other become a
ladder to the moon.

The stars fall to the Earth from the teary eyes of God.
The beginning seems to have no end.
The end seems to have no beginning.

In a world full of liars, a madman is the only one who speaks the truth.

Around this corner of despair, a rainbow shares its colors with a black and white world.

Dancing In Italy

Wolfgang Amadeus Mozart brought sorrow and joy to life.
An orchestra performs his violin concerto in the golden
shadow of the Renaissance.
What a sight to see, violins and pianos singing in Italy.

Wine, the scarlet mistake, the white miracle.
While David drinks wine from a glass mistake soon to
become a glass miracle, lightning strikes a slab of marble.

The pages of tomorrow, sculpted by the black thunder called
inspiration, painting a picture of day dancing with night.

Gladiators clash and gladiators battle in the Roman
Coliseum, clashing inside a massive Roman dome.

Italians watch and Romans cheer as tournaments of strength
and courage clash in the Coliseum of ancient Rome.

In this brief shining moment, the past was painted by the
future into an Italian paradise we would someday see.

Someday we will dance the night away.
Someday we will dance in Italy.